THIS BOOK BELONGS TO

www.sardinecanbooks.com

To: Addy!
Enjoy - !
Nancy Gebhardt

"Family School"

How Much Trouble Could a Can of Sardines Get Into?

Velvet Cat
Publishing

BY Nancy Bloy Gebhardt

ILLUSTRATED BY Brett Stokes

For my kids and grandkids, with special thanks to Mom, with love - N.G.

For Mom and Dad - B.S.

Text copyright © 2011 by Nancy Bloy Gebhardt
Illustrations copyright © 2011 by Brett Stokes
All rights reserved, including the right of reproduction in whole or in part in any form.
Velvet Cat logo and King Triton Sardine can are trademarks of
Velvet Cat Publishing

Published by Velvet Cat Publishing
P.O. Box 2408
Fallbrook, CA 92088
www.sardinecanbooks.com

Library of Congress Control Number: 2011923124

Gebhardt, Nancy Bloy, 2011
How Much Trouble Could a Can of Sardines Get Into? /
Nancy Bloy Gebhardt, illustrated by Brett Stokes
First printing 2011

Summary: What happens when a can of sardines decide it's time to
get out of the can? Adventures ensue.
ISBN 978-0-615-42635-8 (softcover)
(1. Sardines - Fiction, 2. Sardine can - Fiction, 3. Bus - Fiction,
4. Farm - Fiction, 5. Park - Fiction)
I. Stokes, Brett, ill. II Title.

Printed in China

Did you ever wonder what it would be like to be a sardine and live inside a sardine can? Once in a while, the tight space in the can must be too much, even for the most well behaved fish. Oh, I think I hear them talking!

"Stop it Bobby, you're squishing me!"
"Well your fin is poking me."
"I can't breathe!"
"I'm too hot!"
"It's dark in here."
"I can't feel my fins!"
"It's stinky in here. Bobby did you..."
"Why does everybody always blame me?"
"'Cause it usually IS you."
"That's it. I'm out of here!"

Bobby popped out of the can. He was tired of being cooped up with a bunch of whiners. Not to be left behind, the other fish popped out too.

"Wow! There's lots of room out here." said Blake.

"Hey Bridget, can you give me a fin with this box of spaghetti noodles?" Bobby asked. "What are you going to do?" asked Bridget, curious. "Just help me get this end open and I'll show you".

The woman of the house was just taking the dog out for a walk. The fish all scurried after them out the door, to the elevator. As the huge door slid open they scrambled inside. "It's crowded in here" whispered Hailee. "We should have stayed in the can", added Hannah.

Then the elevator door opened with a "whoosh" and all the shoes hurried out. At the end of a long hallway the fish met a very large revolving door that never stopped turning.

"Now what do we do?" asked Bridget. She was all for the adventure, but this looked dangerous. "On my mark we're going to make a run for it" said Bobby. "But be very careful. We have to stick together". "O.K., ready? One, two, three – GO!" Thank goodness they timed it just right, and made a beeline out the door to the street.

"That was weely scawy!" exclaimed Valerie, the littlest sardine. She still had a little trouble with her "rrrs", but they all understood what she meant as they stood there holding their fins to their chests. That was a close one!

Outside on the sidewalk they were once again surrounded by a crowd of shuffling feet. This time Hailee held back the urge to complain just long enough to spot a bus across the street. "Hey guys, look. Maybe if we get on that bus over there we can find a place, with wide open spaces, where a few fish could have some breathing room".

"The bus is crowded too!" Will complained.

It was full of kids and older people, all excited to be going somewhere. They wondered where?

When they passed the fire station with the big red fire trucks, Bobby said "Wow! Can we stop there?"

The next thing you know the bus stopped at a big park with wide open spaces. "This is it!" they told each other as they hopped out of the bus and landed on the soft green grass. Hannah had a great time bumping a soccer ball around with her head. The others took turns rolling down the hill. They were just the right shape for that. "It tickles!" giggled Valerie.

They played, laughed, and took long, lazy naps. When they woke up, they were surprised to find that they were surrounded by lots of people with blankets and picnic baskets. And it was getting dark.

All of a sudden the sky exploded with bright lights and the people on the blankets shouted with delight. The scared fish jumped into the nearest picnic basket. "It's crowded in here!" moaned CJ, but they decided to make the best of it and settled in.

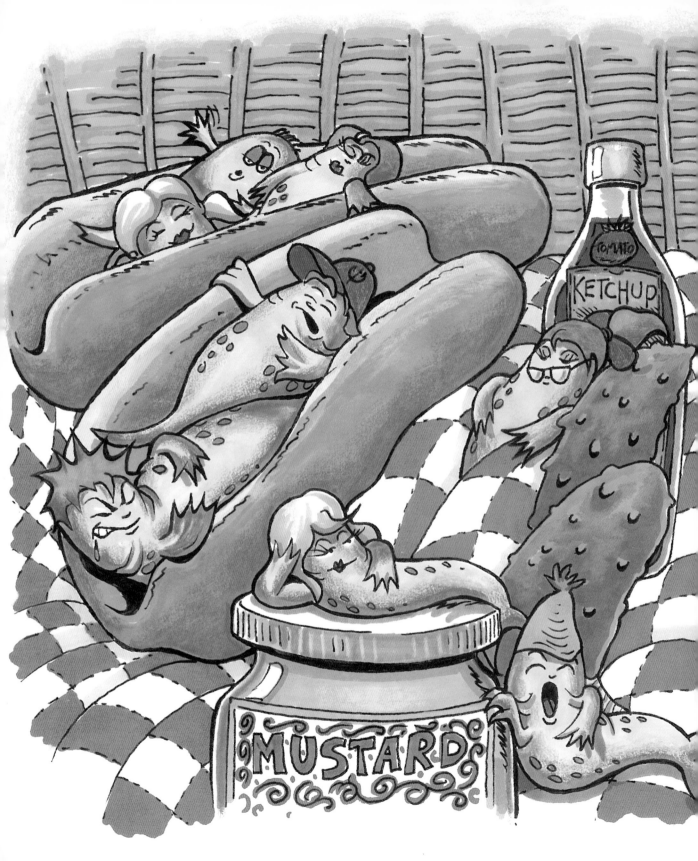

They didn't remember falling asleep. When they woke up the sardines discovered that they were on the bus again, and happy to be going home, except… "This isn't the way home!" Bridget exclaimed. The bus was headed in the wrong direction! Instead of tall buildings and honking horns, all they saw were wide open spaces. Little Valerie started to cry, but Hailee patted her head with her fin. "Maybe this won't be so bad". "We did want more room to wiggle our fins".

The bus stopped at a farm and all the fish hopped out. The sun was just coming up and starting to brighten the early morning sky. Suddenly a rooster crowed and scared the living daylights out of the fish. They had never heard that sound before in the big city!

They scrambled into the barn right in the middle of milking time. The cows were lined up in a tight row, shifting and mooing, waiting their turn to be milked. "It's crowded in here!" Hannah cried.

They scurried out of the barn and landed PLOP, right in the pig pen, squirming in the mud. The pigs gave them a casual look, and went on eating slop and feeding their babies.

Just then the rooster crowed again, which sent the sardines flying into the nearby chicken coop for safety. "Never saw flying fish before" grunted one lazy pig to the other, in pig talk, of course.

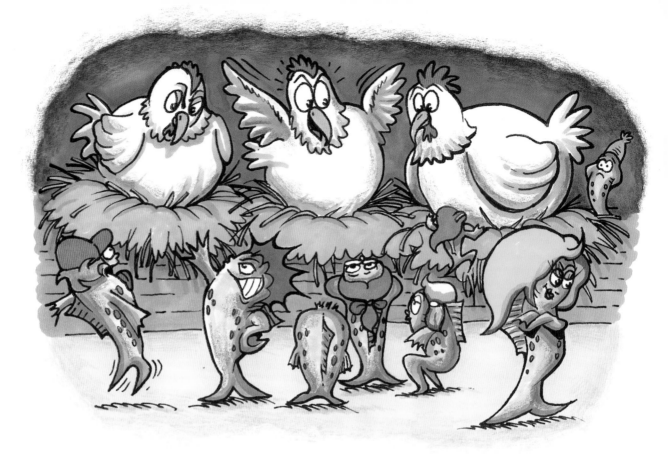

"Whoa" said Blake. "Look at all these chickens". "It's crowded in here!" the other fish complained. This time, when the rooster crowed for the last scary time, all the sardines jumped under the nearest hen. It was dark under there, and it kind of felt like home, until they noticed something *fishy*.

There were lots of eyes staring at each other. Will started counting and realized that there were a lot more than eight sardines in their hiding place. "Soft, fuzzy chicks!" exclaimed Hannah. "Can I keep one, Bobby?"

All the sardines were relieved, until they started sneezing from feathers tickling their noses. "AAAH CHOO!" As soon as mama hen realized something was very wrong under there, she started clucking and fretting. She jumped up and scared the poor little fish again. They made a beeline for the door, popped through, and came face to face with the rooster! "Yikes!" yelled Will.

The sardines were not sure how they made it back on that bus so fast, but they did know it was TIME TO GO HOME! They snoozed on the bus trip back to the city. Hopping off at the right street, they wiggled back through the traffic, through the revolving door, down the long hallway, into the elevator, up into the cabinet, and right back into their can.

As they cranked the lid back to close it, all the sardines agreed it was good to be home safe. It was a fun adventure, but they realized that they didn't really mind being tucked in close to each other.

They would have enjoyed a nice long nap, until Bridget said "Has anyone seen Bobby?"

THE END

For Now!

"Family School"